To Katherine
The real creator of Madelyn and Lydia

—K.F.

To Lana, David, and Jackie

—P.M.

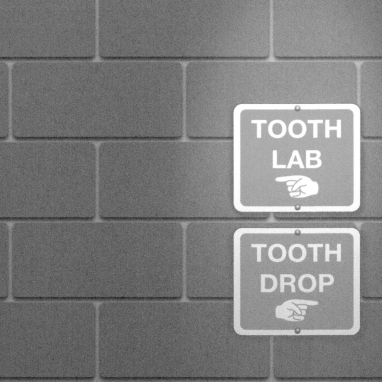

TOOTH FAIRIES AND JETPACKS

Published by Wonderstruck Press, 89 Commander Black Drive, Oradell, NJ 07649

ISBN: 978-0-9997360-0-5

First Printing: February, 2018

First Edition: February, 2018

Tooth Fairies
and
Jetpacks

Written by
Kurt Fried

Illustrations by
Patrick Meehan

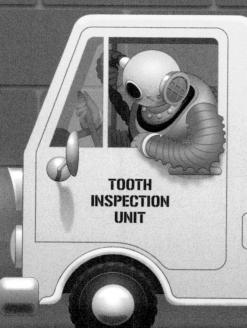

Dear Tooth Fairy,
I lost another tooth! Can I have some fairy dust?
Is that how you fly? I know I'm probably
getting a quarter, but could I have a
gajillion dollars instead?

Thanks,
Madelyn

Dear Madelyn:

Thank you for the lovely incisor. To answer
your questions,

1. I don't use any fairy dust to fly, and so,
   no you can't have any.

2. I use a jetpack.

3. And no, I won't bring you a gajillion dollars
   next time. A gajillion isn't a number.

Yours always,
The Tooth Fairy

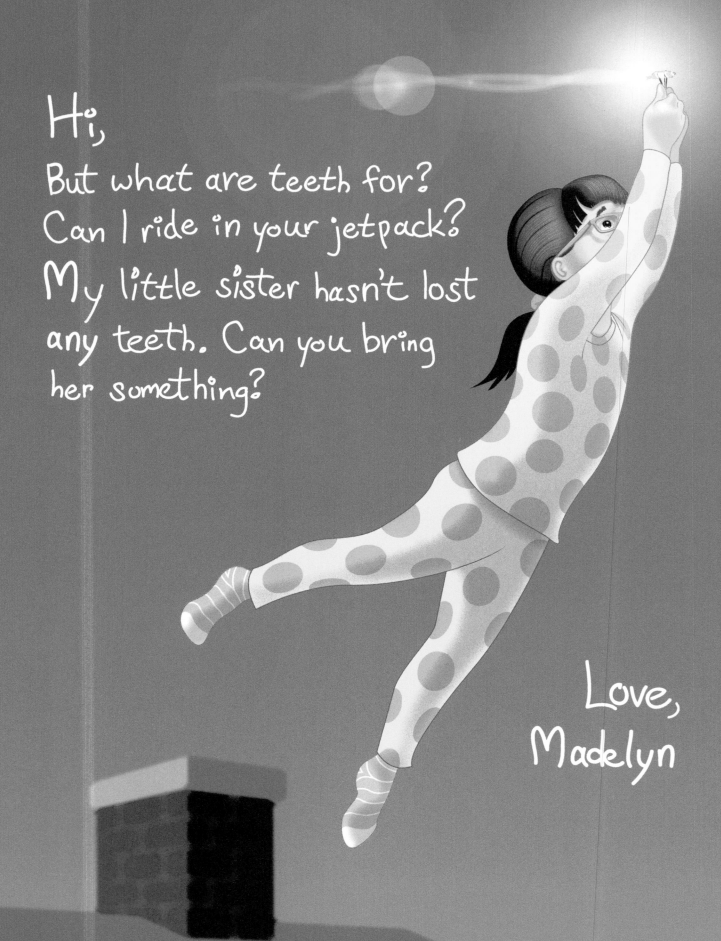

Hi,
But what are teeth for?
Can I ride in your jetpack?
My little sister hasn't lost
any teeth. Can you bring
her something?

Love,
Madelyn

Dear Madelyn—

Those are much more interesting questions. What do we do with the teeth? We study them. We're scientists. All tooth fairies are. There are special things inside the teeth called "stem cells." These cells can do cool things. I learn a lot from them.

No, you can't ride in the jetpack. It's too small for you, and that's one of the first rules we're taught: no kids in jetpacks.

It's sweet to see you caring about your little sister. I left you an extra coin to give her.

The Tooth Fairy

Hi Lydia,

I haven't written a lot of these notes. My name is Toothetina. Tina for short. I'm just starting out as a fairy. Your sister's fairy, Hildegard Saarsgard Beauregard, is my teacher.

She lets me call her Miss Hildie to save time. She shows me how to carry money so much bigger than me. How do you spend money that big? And she teaches me how to hide, but I am not good at hiding. I make a lot of noise and can't blend in like Miss Hildie can.

Your very own fairy,
Tina

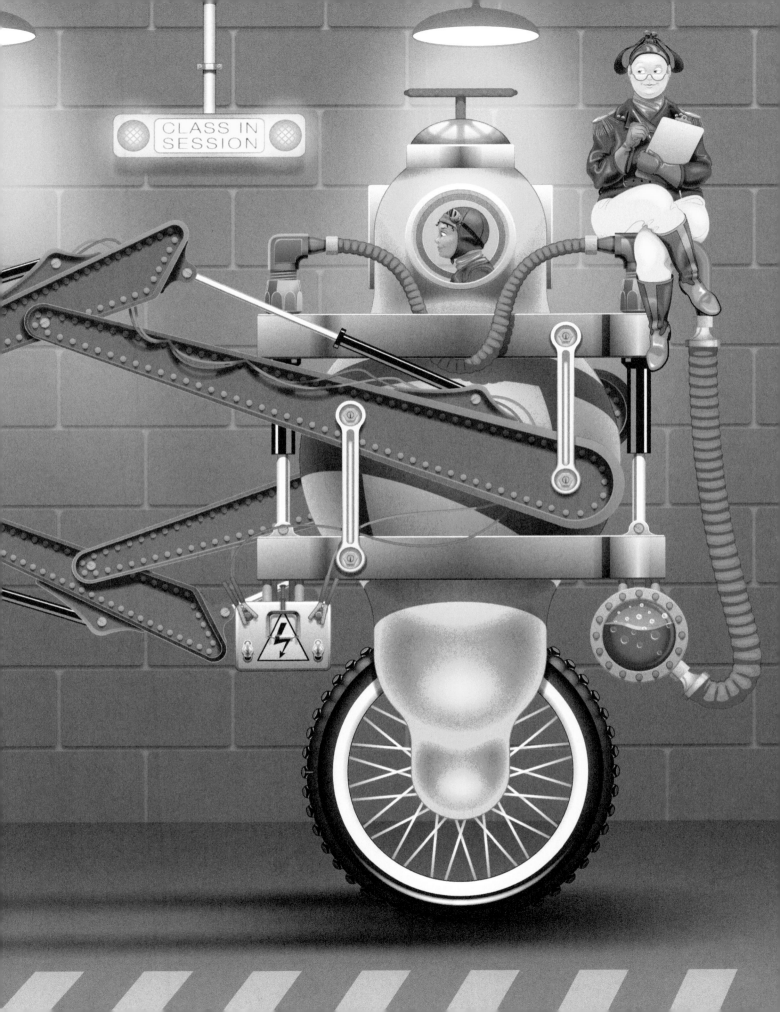

Hi Hildie,
Lydia's fairy told us your name.
Can you meet me in the closet?
I really want to meet you.

Love,
Madelyn

Hi Madelyn,

Tina wasn't supposed to use our real names. Sorry, no we can't meet in the closet. It's not good for fairies and humans to meet face-to-face. But since Tina is telling secrets...

You know that time of year when fireflies come out just as it's getting dark? That's when we take a chance and fly around in the open. Our jetpacks light up, but it's OK, because we hide among the fireflies. I've never gotten caught, but sometimes it's been close. So when you see fireflies, the one you don't catch might be me.

Love,
The Tooth Fairy
(Hildie)

Tina Fairy
I LOVE fireflies. I am going to
catcH you.
Lydia

Hi Madelyn,

I made a mistake. I shouldn't have said anything about the fireflies. Now I can't find Tina. I'm worried. I didn't tell you why we study the teeth. Because of people germs. There are germs we get from people that make us get sick. We are trying to make medicine so we don't get sick around people. That's why we don't let you see us, and that's why we have you put the teeth under a pillow, so we stay away from your faces. If Lydia caught her, I'm afraid Tina will get sick. I'm looking everywhere, but if you see anything, let me know.

Worried,
Hildie

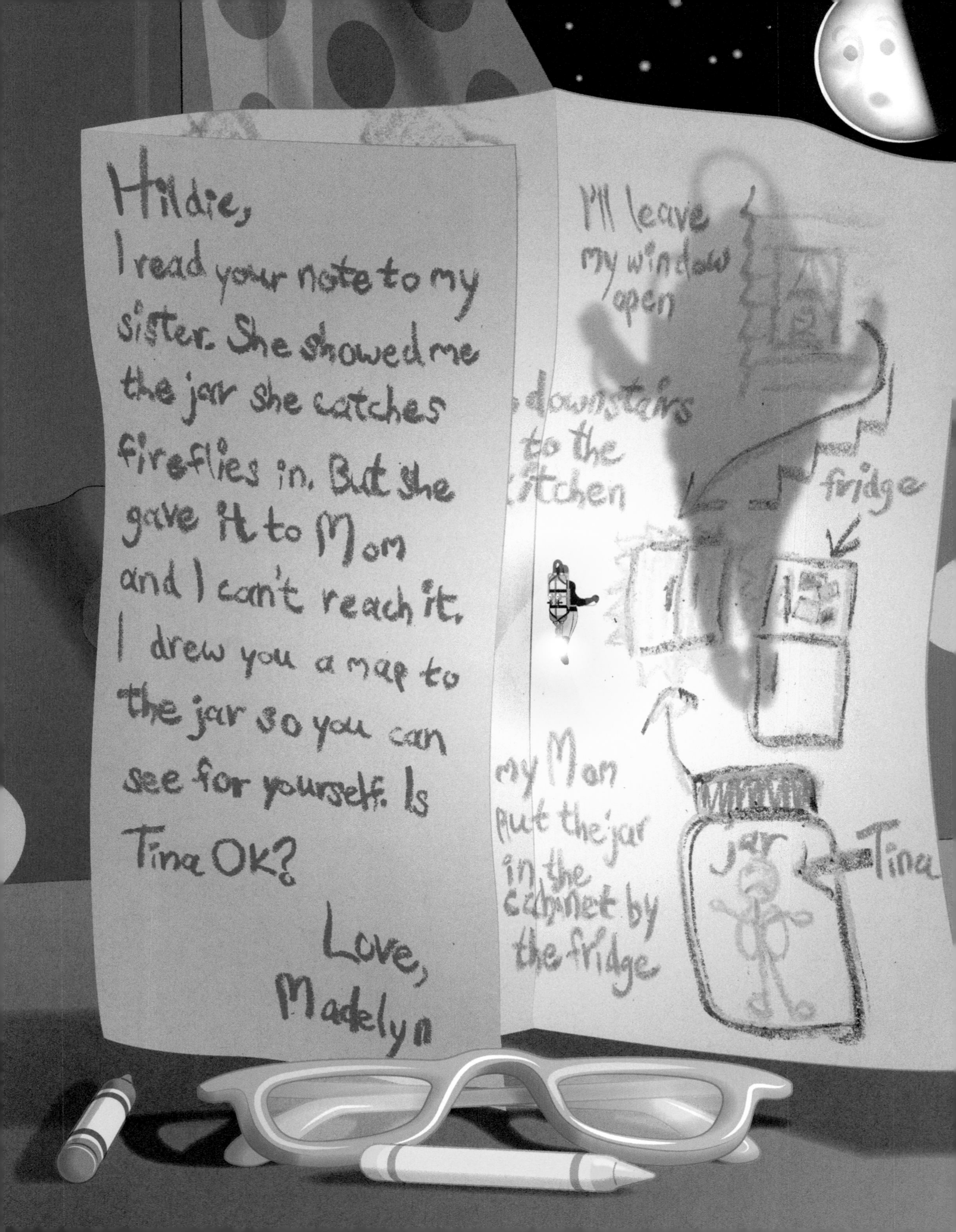
Hildie,
I read your note to my sister. She showed me the jar she catches fireflies in. But she gave it to Mom and I can't reach it. I drew you a map to the jar so you can see for yourself. Is Tina OK?
Love,
Madelyn
I'll leave my window open
downstairs to the
fridge
my Mom put the jar in the cabinet by the fridge
jar
Tina

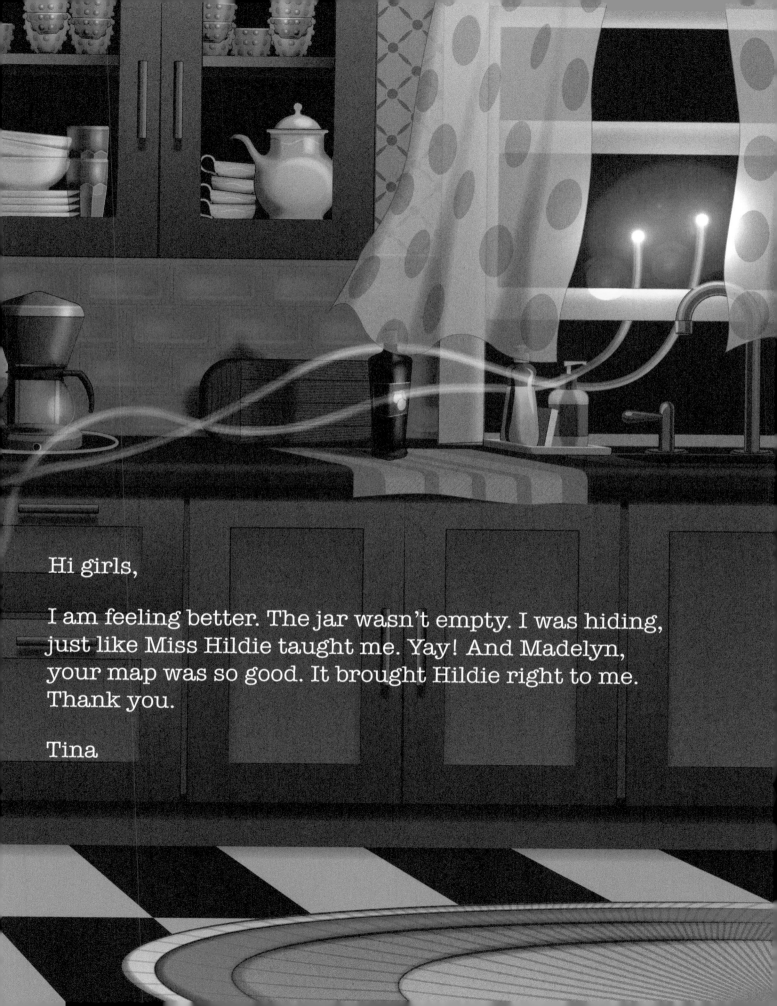

Hi girls,

I am feeling better. The jar wasn't empty. I was hiding, just like Miss Hildie taught me. Yay! And Madelyn, your map was so good. It brought Hildie right to me. Thank you.

Tina

Dear Madelyn and Lydia,

I thought you would want to know that Toothetina has graduated and is now a full-fledged Tooth Fairy. She learned valuable lessons from you, like staying calm in scary situations and not flying so close to the ground where kids could grab you. She's growing up to be a smart, mature young fairy. I'm proud of her.

Love,
Hildie

Dear Hildie & Tina,
We're so happy about
Tina. We want to help with finding
medicine, so we can play with you. So far,
I've made some green, bubbly stuff. I'll leave
some under my pillow and you can see if it helps.

Love,
Madelyn
and
Lydia

Hey girls,

I was working on the jetpack's engine, and I think I figured out how a human could use it. Who wants to go for a ride?

Toothetina, Professional Tooth Fairy

The end!

Kurt Fried has enjoyed both writing and science his whole life. He has an MFA in creative writing from American University. He lives with his family in New Jersey.

Patrick Meehan is an artist and illustrator who lives with his family in Brooklyn, NY, and who always makes sure to brush his teeth twice a day.

Did you enjoy reading this?
Want to know when there will be more?
Let us know at:

toothfairiesandjetpacks@gmail.com

CPSIA information can be obtained
at www.ICGtesting.com
Printed in the USA
BVOW07*1709120218
507227BV00003B/2/P

9 780999 736005